D1360718

SNOW WHITE
and the
THREE GIANTS

By Cherie Gosling

Illustrated by Alan Batson and Studio Iboix

A Random House PICTUREBACK® Book

Random House 🏠 New York

randomhousekids.com
ISBN 978-0-7364-3734-9
Printed in the United States of America
10 9 8 7 6 5 4 3 2 1

One day, Snow White was on her way to the Dwarfs' cottage when she accidentally took a wrong turn.

She arrived at a very different cottage.

"Oh, my!" exclaimed Snow White when she stepped inside. Instead of a neat row of seven little chairs, she saw three enormous chairs!

Instead of her little oven in the
cozy kitchen where she loved to cook,
she found a fire roaring and crackling
in an enormous hearth.

Snow White also discovered an enormous dining table.

Just then, the ground began to shake!

"Oh, no!" she gasped.

The front door opened with a groan, and three of the tallest people Snow White had ever seen entered the cottage.

They lumbered straight toward her!

What should I do? she wondered.

Snow White cleared her throat and stepped into view.

"Excuse me," she said. The giants jumped back in surprise.

One knocked over his chair.

"You startled us," said the largest giant. "We don't get visitors very often."

"But now that you're here," said the smallest giant, "you should join us for dinner."

The smallest giant helped her climb onto his chair.
"You'll need some cushions," he said.

"And here are a small plate and a glass," said the
middle-sized giant.

Snow White and the giants talked and
laughed while they shared a lovely meal.

The next day, Snow White
told the Dwarfs about
her new friends.

"G-g-giants?" stammered Bashful.

Sleepy yawned. "Aren't they dangerous?"

"Not at all," said Snow White. "They're very friendly."

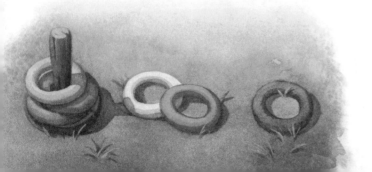

"You can't trust anyone tall!" said Grumpy.

"But I'm taller than you, and you trust me," Snow White pointed out. Grumpy scowled and crossed his arms.

"Well, you'll just have to meet them," Snow White said.

That evening, Snow White carefully addressed ten party invitations and made a list of the delicious food she'd prepare. All she needed was a game to get everyone laughing.

When the Dwarfs and the giants arrived on the day
of the party, Snow White announced to her guests,
"We're going to play a game called Snap! I'll point out
something about me and, if it's true for you, shout
SNAP! Then it's someone else's turn."

"I'll start," said Snow White, thinking for a moment.
"I have two eyes."

"SNAP!" yelled the giants.

"SNAP!" yelled the Dwarfs.

Bashful was up next.

"Um, I have two ears," said Bashful. As he spoke, both ears turned bright red.

"SNAP!" called the giants.

"SNAP!" called the Dwarfs.

It was the largest giant's turn next.

"I have one nose," he said. He pointed to his very large nose.

"SNAP!" shouted the giants.

"SNAP!" shouted the Dwarfs.

"I guess we have a lot in common after all,"
Grumpy muttered.

"Yes, you do!" said Snow White.
"And there's one more thing you have
in common: you are all my friends!"

"Yup, yup!" giggled Gus. "Let's dance, Cinderelly!"
Cinderella gladly joined her friends on the dance
floor. It was a perfect day!

"Let's celebrate!" cheered Jaq.

One of the girls led Cinderella to where the rest of the villagers were already dancing. The girls loved the way their new dresses spun and twirled!

Soon Cinderella gave each of the five girls
a pretty new dress.

"Thank you!" they cried together.

"Thanks to you all," replied Cinderella, "these are
some of the best dresses I've ever made!"

Tweet, tweet, tweet, sang the birds as they helped
Cinderella sew together the bows and fabric.

"Take some blue fabric from mine!"
said another girl.

"Here's some yellow fabric," added another.
"And here's some pink," added one more.

As Cinderella started to put the new dress together, the girls found more ways to share.

"You can use some purple bows from my dress," said one girl.

Swish, swoosh, swish.

The cloth rustled when Jaq, Gus, and the girls gathered it up.

Snip, snip, snip!
Cinderella carefully cut some
ruffles off each dress.

Cinderella and the girls
got to work right away.

"What if we shared a part of each dress?" asked one girl. "Then maybe there would be enough cloth to make another one."

"That's a wonderful idea!" exclaimed Cinderella. "Would you like to help?"

Cinderella stepped down from the carriage.
"To thank you all for inviting me," she said,
"I wanted to surprise you with new dresses.
But I'm afraid I've only made four."

"There must be a new family in the village,"
said Cinderella. "What should we do?"

When they reached the village, the little
girls ran out to greet them.

"Here they come!" squealed Gus.

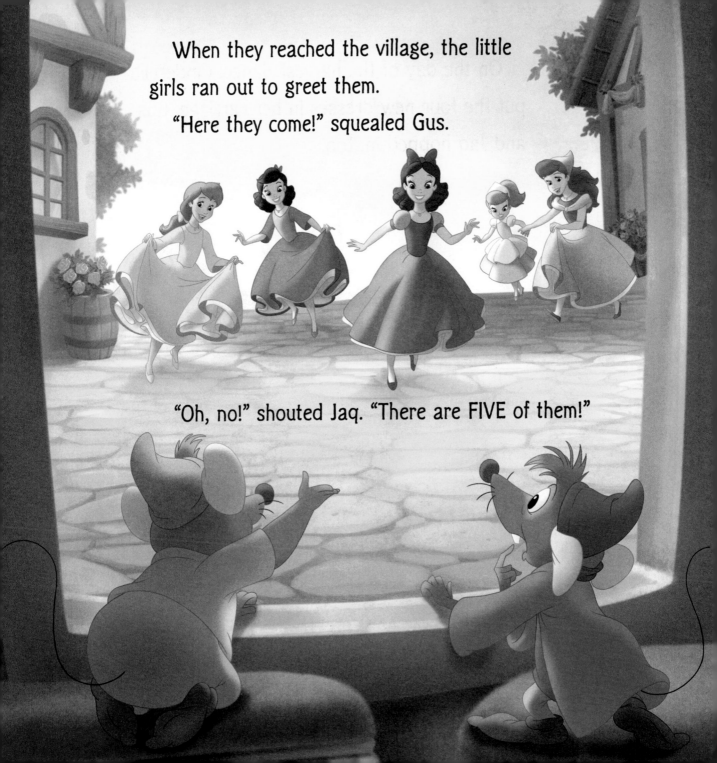

"Oh, no!" shouted Jaq. "There are FIVE of them!"

On the day of the harvest dance, Cinderella put the four new dresses in her carriage. Gus and Jaq hopped in, too.

The first dress was done—and it was beautiful!
Now she just had to make three more.

She cut out the pattern.

Then she sewed all the pieces together.

Cinderella started working on the first dress right away.
She laid out the fabric.

"That's a great idea!" squeaked Jaq.

Gus clapped. "Those little girls will feel so, so special!"

This year, Cinderella wanted to do something special for the villagers.

"I know!" she said to her mouse friends. "There are four little girls in the village. I'll make them each a new dress."

Cinderella was excited to get an invitation to the harvest dance in her village. It was her favorite event of the year!

Disney PRINCESS

Cinderella's Best Creations

By Cherie Gosling

Illustrated by Alan Batson and the Disney Storybook Art Team

A Random House PICTUREBACK® Book

Random House 🏠 New York

randomhousekids.com
ISBN 978-0-7364-3734-9
Printed in the United States of America
10 9 8 7 6 5 4 3 2 1